Ladybird Readers

Hansel and Gretel

Series Editor: Sorrel Pitts
Text adapted by Sorrel Pitts
Illustrated by Marina Le Ray

LADYBIRD BOOKS

UK | USA | Canada | Ireland | Australia
India | New Zealand | South Africa

Ladybird Books is part of the Penguin Random House group of companies
whose addresses can be found at global.penguinrandomhouse.com.
www.penguin.co.uk   www.puffin.co.uk   www.ladybird.co.uk

Penguin
Random House
UK

First published 2017
001

Copyright © Ladybird Books Ltd, 2017

Printed in China

A CIP catalogue record for this book is available from the British Library

ISBN: 978-0-241-29861-9

All correspondence to
Ladybird Books
Penguin Random House Children's
80 Strand, London WC2R 0RL

MIX
Paper from
responsible sources
FSC® C018179

Ladybird Readers

Hansel and Gretel

Hansel

Gretel

father

aunt

witch

forest

path

cut wood

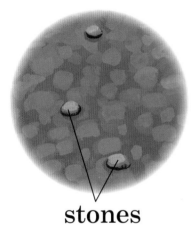

stones

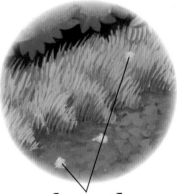

bread

cage

oven

Hansel and Gretel lived with their father and aunt in a little house near a forest. Their father cut wood to get money, but he was very poor. They were all very hungry.

One day, Hansel and Gretel's father said, "There is no more money. There is no more food for us to eat."

"Then, Hansel and Gretel cannot live here," said their aunt. "We must leave them in the forest."

"No," said their father. "We can't do that."

"But we must do it," their aunt said.

Hansel and Gretel were in their bedroom, but they heard everything.

"I have an idea," said Hansel, and he went outside to get some stones.

The next day, they all
went into the forest.

Hansel put the stones
on the path.

"Wait here," said Hansel and Gretel's father. "We want to get some wood."

Hansel and Gretel waited all day. Then, they found all the stones on the path, and walked home.

Hansel and Gretel's father was happy to see them, but their aunt was very angry.

"There isn't enough food for all of us," she said. "We must take Hansel and Gretel back into the forest."

"No!" said their father.
"I don't want to do that."

"We have to do it," said their aunt. "This time, they mustn't come home."

Hansel and Gretel's aunt closed the door and used the key. Hansel and Gretel couldn't get out of the house. Hansel couldn't find any stones.

The next day, they all went back into the forest. This time, Hansel left some bread on the path.

"Wait here," said Hansel and Gretel's father. "We want to get some wood."

Hansel and Gretel waited all day. Then, they looked for the bread on the path.

But there was no bread. "The birds ate it," said Gretel sadly. Hansel and Gretel couldn't get home.

Hansel and Gretel went into the forest. They walked for many hours.

In the middle of the forest, they found a house made of candies and cake. They wanted to eat it.

A witch lived in the house made of candies and cake. She wanted to eat Hansel and Gretel.

She put Hansel in a cage, and gave him lots of food.

"I want him to get fat," said the witch. "Then, I want to cook him in my fire, and eat him."

"Where is your fire?" said Gretel.

"Here," said the witch.
She showed the oven to Gretel.

"I can't see the fire," said Gretel.

The witch opened the oven door.

"No, I can't see the fire,"
said Gretel.

The witch opened the oven door as much as she could.

Gretel pushed her into the oven, and closed the door!

Gretel opened the cage.

"Look at all this money," she said. "We can take this home, and buy food with it."

Hansel and Gretel walked for many hours, and then they found their house.

Their father was very happy to see them.

"Your aunt left," he said. "She doesn't live here now."

Hansel and Gretel lived with their father for many years. They were very happy in their little house near the forest.

Activities

The key below describes the skills practiced in each activity.

 Spelling and writing

 Reading

 Speaking

Critical thinking

Preparation for the Cambridge Young Learners Exams

1 Look and read. Choose the correct words, and write them on the lines.

| forest | Gretel | hungry | poor |

1 The girl in the story who is Hansel's sister. _Gretel_

2 A place which has many trees. _____

3 People who do not have money are this. _____

4 People who do not have food are this. _____

2 Look and read. Write *yes* or *no*.

Hansel and Gretel lived with their father and aunt in a little house near a forest. Their father cut wood to get money, but he was very poor. They were all very hungry.

1 Did Hansel and Gretel live with their father?

 yes

2 Did Hansel and Gretel's aunt live with them?

3 Was their house in a town?

4 Did Hansel and Gretel's father have a lot of money?

3 Find the words.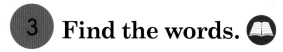

curcagebafcuteeforestlrpnovenouvpathshowoodkniwitchrl

cage
wood
oven
cut
path
witch
forest

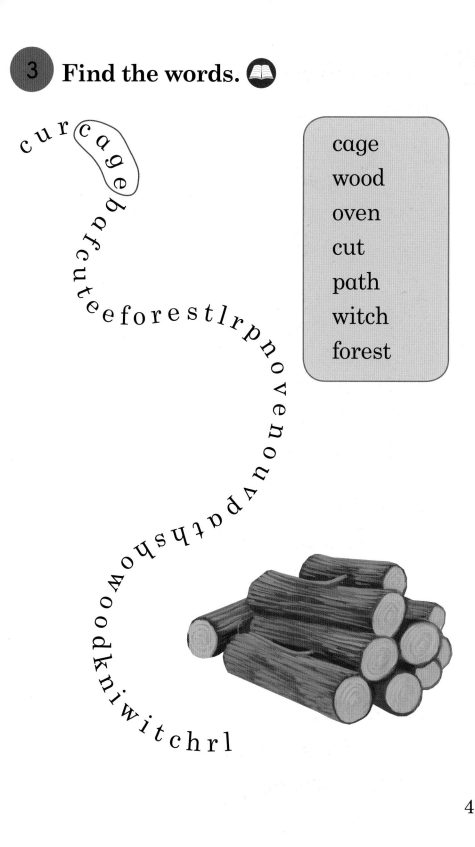

49

4 Look at the letters. Write the words. 📖 ✏️

1 (l a s n e H)

___Hansel___ and Gretel were
in their bedroom.

2 (r h d e a)

They _____ everything
their aunt said.

3 (a i e d)

"I have an _____," said Hansel

4 (o i d e u t s)

Hansel went _____.

5 Look and read. Put a ✓ or a X
in the boxes.

The next day, they all
went into the forest.

Hansel put the stones
on the path.

1 The next day, Hansel and
Gretel went into the forest
with their father and aunt. ✓

2 Hansel put stones on the path. ☐

3 Hansel and Gretel's father
saw the stones on the path. ☐

4 Hansel and Gretel were
very happy. ☐

6 Work with a friend. You are Gretel, and your friend is Hansel. Ask and answer the questions.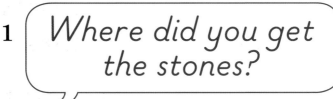

"Wait here," said Hansel and Gretel's father. "We want to get some wood."

Hansel and Gretel waited all day. Then, they found all the stones on the path, and walked home.

1 *Where did you get the stones?*

I got them from outside our house.

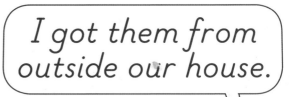

2 Where are Father and Aunt taking us?

3 What are you putting on the path?

4 Why are you doing this?

7 Match the two parts of the sentences.

1 "Wait here,"

2 "We want

3 Hansel and Gretel

4 They found

a the stones on the path.

b waited all day.

c said Hansel and Gretel's father.

d to get some wood."

8 **Look and read. Write the correct words on the lines.** 📖 ✏️

happy   forest   enough   angry

1 Hansel and Gretel's father was

_____happy_____ to see them.

2 But their aunt was very

_____.

3 "There isn't _____ food for all of us," she said.

4 "We must take Hansel and Gretel back into the _____."

9 Read the story. Choose the correct words and write them next to 1—4.

1	although	so	because
2	had to	has to	must
3	come	to come	came
4	close	closed	closes

Hansel and Gretel's father was very

sad [1] _because_ he did not want

to take his children back into the forest.

"We [2] _____ do it," said their

aunt. "This time they mustn't

[3] _____ home." Hansel and

Gretel's aunt [4] _____ the door.

10 Talk about the two pictures with a friend. How are they different? Use the words in the box. 💬

inside   sad   dark   happy
forest   house   father

In picture a, the children are sad.

In picture b, the children are happy.

Circle the correct words.

1 The next day, Hansel and Gretel went back into the **house. / forest.**

2 This time, Hansel left some **stones / bread** on the path.

3 "Wait here," said their **aunt. / father.**

4 "We want to get some **wood," / stones,"** their father said.

12 Do the crossword. 📖 ✏️

Down

1 Hansel put these on the path.

2 Hansel and Gretel's . . . cut wood.

Across

2 Hansel and Gretel's father took them here.

3 This person did not want to live with Hansel and Gretel.

4 Hansel and Gretel were . . . when they couldn't get home.

13 Choose the correct answers.

1 Hansel and Gretel . . . all day.

   a wait   **b** waited

2 Then, they . . . for the bread on the path.

   a looked   **b** look

3 The birds . . .

   a eat it.   **b** ate it.

4 Hansel and Gretel . . . get home.

   a couldn't   **b** can't

14 **Match the words to the pictures.**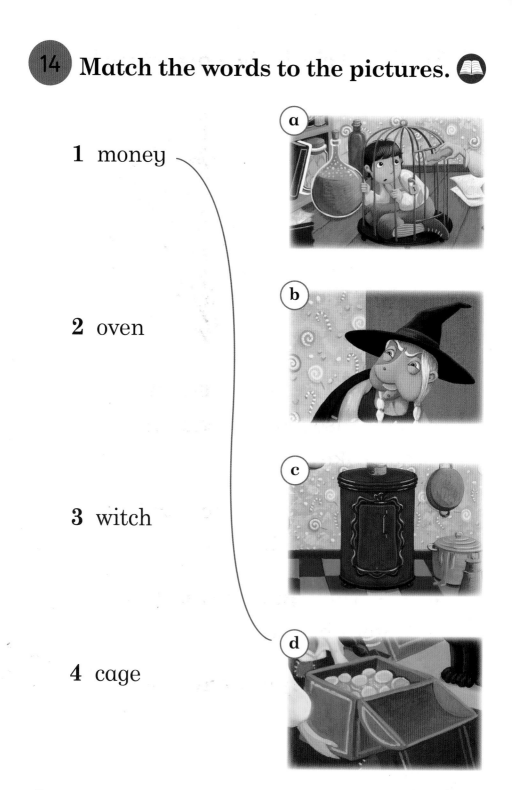

1 money

2 oven

3 witch

4 cage

15 **Read and circle the correct verbs.**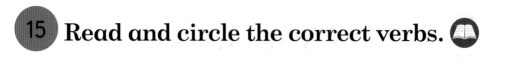

1 A witch (lived)/ living in the house made of candies and cake.

2 The witch wanted to **ate / eat** Hansel and Gretel.

3 The witch **putting / put** Hansel in a cage.

4 The witch **give / gave** him lots of food.

16 Order the story. Write 1—5. 📖

_____ The witch showed Gretel her oven, but Gretel couldn't see the fire.

_____ Gretel pushed the witch into the oven, and closed the door!

_____ The witch wanted to eat Hansel.

__1__ Hansel and Gretel found a house made of candies and cake.

_____ The witch opened the oven door as much as she could.

17 **Read the questions. Write the answers.** 📖 ✏️ ⬠ ❓

1 Who were poor at the beginning of the story, but were rich at the end?

Hansel, Gretel, and
their father.

2 Why did Gretel say, "I can't see the fire."?

_____

_____

3 Did Hansel and Gretel want their aunt to come back home? Why? / Why not?

_____

_____

Level 3

Sharks
978-0-241-25382-3

The Jungle Book
978-0-241-25383-0

The Red Knight
978-0-241-25384-7

The Elves and the Shoemaker
978-0-241-25385-4

Rapunzel
978-0-241-28394-3

Great Buildings
978-0-241-28400-1

Minibeasts
978-0-241-28404-9

Puss in Boots
978-0-241-28407-0

Jack and the Beanstalk
978-0-241-28397-4

Hansel and Gretel
978-0-241-29861-9

The Talent Show
978-0-241-29859-6

A Great Night!
978-0-241-29863-3

Bumblebee and the Rock Concert
978-0-241-29867-1

Where Animals Live
978-0-241-29868-8

Now you're ready for Level 4!